P9-EDV-834

J
635
Dad   85-375
  Daddona, Mark
    Hoe, hoe, hoe, watch my
  garden grow

DATE DUE

                                    85-375
  J   Daddona, Mark
  635
  Dad   Hoe, hoe, hoe, watch
          my garden grow

DATE DUE	BORROWER'S NAME
JUL 11 1988	979
APR 20 1990	2130
MAR 28 1992	270

Irene Ingle Public Library
P. O. Box 679
Wrangell, Alaska   99929

HOE, HOE, HOE,

Watch

My Garden Grow

Written & illustrated by

MARK DADDONA

▲▲ **ADDISON-WESLEY**

Irene Ingle Public Library
P.O. Box 679
Wrangell, Alaska 99929

Text copyright © 1980 by Mark F. Daddona
Illustrations copyright © 1980 by Mark F. Daddona
All Rights Reserved
Addison-Wesley Publishing Company, Inc.
Reading, Massachusetts 01867
Printed in the United States of America
ABCDEFGHIJK-WZ-89876543210

Library of Congress Cataloging in Publication Data

Daddona, Mark,
  Hoe, hoe, hoe, watch my garden grow.
  SUMMARY: A guide for growing vegetables for the
beginning gardener.
  1. Vegetable gardening—Juvenile literature.
[1. Vegetable gardening. 2. Gardening] I. Title.
SB324.D3   635   79-25039
ISBN 0-201-03079-9
ISBN 0-201-03004-7 pbk.

85-375

TO GRANDMA:
who started me with
gardening when I was ten

TABLE OF CONTENTS

1

WHERE DO I PUT MY GARDEN?

The first problem you have with your first vegetable garden is where to put it. You might say there is no place for a garden so I won't have one. If you have a yard at all, I am sure you can find a place if you look hard enough. There must be a piece of ground just waiting to be made into a garden.

There are a few things to keep in mind when you are looking for a site for your garden.

1. Do not put your garden in the middle of the backyard.

2. Do not put your garden at the bottom of a hill or where puddles form after a rain. Your plants do not know how to swim.

3. Put your garden out of the way, where animals do not tramp.

4. Put it where it will not interfere with your playing area. A ball kicked into the garden could damage a plant.

5. Your garden should be in an area that has at least 6 hours of direct sunlight a day.

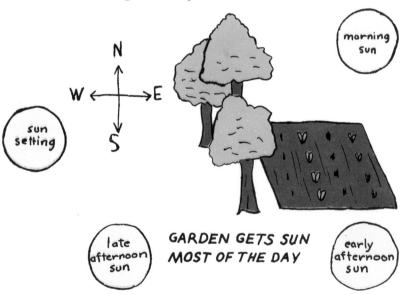

6. Put your vegetable garden away from large trees. They have big roots which will get in the way of your young plants.

7. Most important of all, do not put your vegetable garden west or directly north of any tall trees, or anything else that will cast shadows on it.

You might say, "How do I know what is west or north of tall trees?" or, "How do I know where the shadows are coming from?" Let me explain this to you. The sun rises in the east and sets in the west. You can see where the east and west are by watching the sun in the morning and evening. If you plant your garden to the west of tall trees, it will be shaded in the early part of the day.

If you place your plants to the north of tall trees, the trees will cast shadows on your plants in the middle to late afternoon. Your garden should be planted **3** east or south of anything that casts a shadow.

Now that you have all of these facts about where to put your garden, take a walk around the yard, with your book if you want, and look for a spot that agrees with most of these facts. It will be hard to find the perfect spot. My garden gets too much water in some places, not enough light in others. Just do the best you can when you are choosing a spot for your garden.

4

2

HOW BIG
DO I MAKE
MY GARDEN?

Another problem is how big to make your garden. Most children like to think big and want a large garden at first. Many times this is too much work for the young gardener to handle. He or she soon loses interest and the garden is left unwatered and soon the weeds are bigger than the plants. I don't want this to happen to you.

My first garden was 5 feet by 5 feet. Now it is 25 feet by 25 feet. It is best to start out small. It is good if your garden has extra room around it. This way if you like gardening, you can make it larger each year.

If you are taking care of the garden by yourself, it should be smaller than if the whole family is taking care of it. To start out with, 5 feet by 10 feet is a good size. Maybe even a little bit larger, depending upon how old you are.

A garden about this size can hold five different vegetables. A row each of radishes, beets, lettuce, a few tomato plants, and a couple of summer squash plants all fit nicely in a small garden like this.

If your whole family or more than one person is taking care of the garden, it can be larger. It can be fun if the different members of the family have their own sections to take care of themselves.

3

HOW DO I PREPARE THE GROUND?

If the garden is going to be where grass is now growing, the grass has to be taken out. It can be taken out by hand with a shovel. If you have a large garden, your father or mother might want to rent a roto-tiller. With a roto-tiller you do not have to take out the grass. The tiller grinds it up into small pieces but the small pieces of grass should be raked out or they will start to grow again.

7

The only tools you will need to make your garden are a shovel, rake, wheelbarrow, and maybe a hoe.

The best way to start is to mark off the garden with string. This way you know what grass has to be taken out.

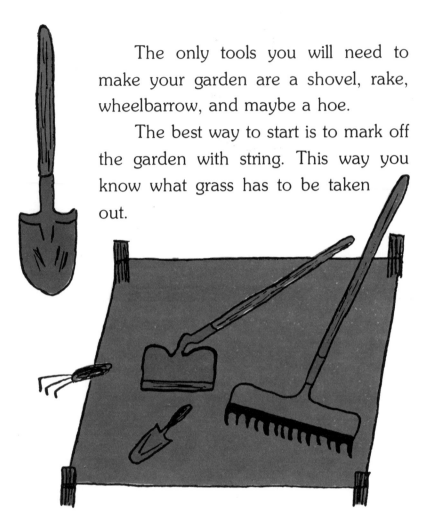

The grass should be cut into squares and taken out one square at a time. The grass is good to use in any bare spots in your yard.

8

Do not take up too much soil with the grass. Take up just enough to hold the grass together. If you dig up too much soil with the grass, you are losing too much topsoil. The topsoil is the best part of the soil.

After all the grass has been taken out, the soil should be turned over with a shovel and

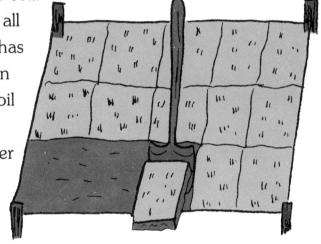

chopped up. A hoe can be used to help chop up the soil. A rake should be used to rake the ground smooth. A rake also helps to get out any large rocks and sticks.

All of the rocks do not have to be taken out of the garden. Only the large

ones have to be removed. The plants will grow around the small rocks.

Is your garden going to be planted where there is no grass? Has a garden been there before? Then you do not have to take out the grass because there will be no grass. But everything else should be done:

1. Turning over the soil
2. Breaking up clumps
3. Raking smooth
4. Removing large stones

10

4

DO I NEED FERTILIZER?

There are two types of fertilizer. *Chemical fertilizer,* which you have to buy, and *organic fertilizer,* which is all around you.

Chemical fertilizer is bought in large boxes and bags. It is made up of different chemicals. These chemicals are needed

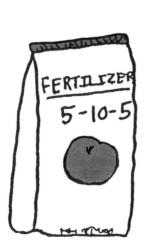
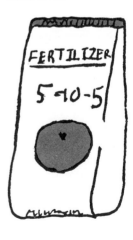

for proper plant growth. Your garden may already have enough of these chemicals. You should not use chemical fertilizer without the supervision of an adult and without reading the directions carefully.

I think organic fertilizer is the best. It is the easiest way to fertilize and the cheapest too. Organic fertilizer is natural. It may be made from grass clippings, straw, hay, peat moss, dry leaves, dead plants, or food leftovers.

Organic fertilizer is sometimes called "compost" because it is made in a com-

post pile. A compost pile, or heap, or bin is a pile of dead plants, leaves, grass, hay, and whatever else you put in it. It is watered from time to time and left for a year to decompose. After a year you can mix it into your soil. Compost is an excellent fertilizer and keeps the soil moist.

Cow and horse manure are also good forms of fertilizer. They can be mixed in the soil as you are turning it over. A little can also be put about an inch under the seeds when you are planting.

5

WHAT SHOULD I PLANT?

This is a question young gardeners often have. First of all, plant only vegetables that you and your family like to eat. If the garden is all yours, you may want to grow what you like to eat. After all you are doing all the work. Each year it is fun to experiment with different vegetables. If one doesn't come out right or if you didn't think you got enough out of it, try something else in its place next year. You might find that you like something that you have always hated.

14

Home-grown vegetables taste so much better than those bought in a store. You might even become a vegetable lover.

Some vegetables are harder to grow than others. Some take longer to mature, more time to become fully grown and ready for you to eat. You might want to start with a vegetable that matures fast rather than something that takes longer. Some vegetables have to be started indoors early in the spring and then transplanted outdoors when the weather is warmer. At first it may be hard to decide what to plant.

These next pages should help you to decide what to grow in your garden.

There are many types of beans to choose from. Bush beans are the short ones. I think they are the best for the beginner to grow. Pole beans need a fence or poles to grow on. Beans are very easy to grow and are in just about every home garden. Bush beans take 50 to 60 days to mature. Pole beans take 60 to 70 days to mature.

BEANS

BEETS

Beets are easy to grow. They can be planted very early in the spring or as soon as the soil is soft enough to dig in. Beets take 55 to 60 days to mature.

Broccoli is not as easy to grow as beans or beets. However, it can be grown without too much trouble. Plants should be started indoors 6 weeks before the planting date. Starting plants indoors will be discussed in another chapter. Broccoli takes 55 to 65 days to mature from the time the

16

plants are set in the garden. This is not from the time the seeds are planted.

Brussels sprouts are like tiny heads of cabbage. They are fun and not too hard to grow. I would wait until my second year of gardening before trying them. Just like broccoli, brussels sprouts should be started indoors. They take 85 days to mature from the time the plants are planted in the garden.

BROCCOLI

Cabbage is hard to grow. It should be started indoors. I would not recommend it for a beginner gardener. Cabbage takes 50 to 70 days to mature for early types and 90 to 100 days to mature for the fall and winter types.

BRUSSELS SPROUTS

Cantaloupe is very hard to grow. I would not recommend it for a beginner gardener. I have been gardening for some time now and still have not been

CABBAGE

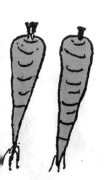

CANTALOUPE

able to grow cantaloupes very well. It should be started indoors 4 weeks before planting outdoors to give it a head start. Cantaloupe takes 80 to 100 days to mature.

Carrots do not like rocky soil. They can be grown without too much trouble if given plenty of room between each plant. They take 70 days to mature.

CARROTS

I would not recommend corn for a small garden or a beginner gardener. It takes up too much room, in my opinion, for the corn it produces, although it is not too hard to grow. Corn takes 70 to 80 days to mature.

CORN

Cucumbers should be planted in hills. They are pretty easy to grow. Cucumbers are climbing plants, so to save space, grow cucumbers along a fence. Grow small types for pickling and larger ones for salads. Cucumbers take 60 days to mature.

18

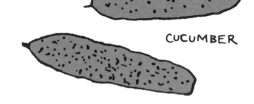

CUCUMBER

Eggplant is hard to grow from seed. It is much easier to buy the plants at a garden center. If you are going to start them indoors, start them 8 to 10 weeks before the last frost. Eggplant takes 70 days to mature from the time the plants are planted.

EGGPLANT

Lettuce is very easy to grow. It is one of the most common vegetables and is found in just about every home garden. Head lettuce takes longer to grow. It should be started indoors 4 weeks before the planting date to give it a head start. Lettuce likes cool weather. It should be planted as early in the spring as the soil can be dug, and again in late summer when the weather cools down. I recommend leaf lettuce very strongly. It is much easier to grow than the head lettuce. Leaf lettuce takes 40 to 50 days to mature.

LETTUCE

19

LETTUCE

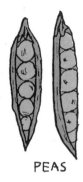

PEAS

Head lettuce takes 80 to 90 days to mature.

Peas are very easy to grow. They like cool weather. Plant them early in the spring. I would recommend peas for the beginner gardener. Peas take 60 to 70 days to mature.

PEPPERS

Peppers are hard to start from seed. You can buy plants or grow them yourself. If you are growing them yourself start them indoors 8 to 10 weeks before planting time. Peppers mature in 70 to 80 days.

Pumpkins are not that hard to grow. I would wait until my second year of gardening before I tried pumpkins if I were you. They need a lot of room and water. They need more room than the young gardener will probably be able to give them. To save space, grow pumpkins along a fence.

PUMPKINS

To grow large pumpkins, pick off all the new flowers after the pumpkins have started. This way all of the water and food goes to the pumpkins already on the vine. Pumpkins take about 100 days to mature.

RADISHES

Radishes are the easiest and fastest vegetables to grow in the garden. Plant them early in the spring and late in August. They like cool weather. Radishes take between 25 and 30 days to mature.

Spinach grows easily in cool weather. It can be planted early in the spring and again in late August. Spinach takes 45 days to mature.

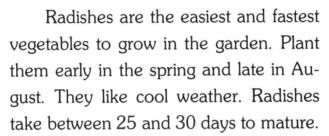

SPINACH

Summer squash is very easy to grow. I would recommend this over winter squash. It is much easier and takes less time to grow. There are many types to choose from. Zucchini and Summer Crookneck are the two most common.

21

SUMMER
SQUASH

Pick squash when they are small. They have fewer seeds, and the plant will produce more this way. Summer squash takes about 50 days to mature.

Winter squash takes longer and is much harder to grow than summer squash. Common ones are Butternut and Acorn. Winter squash can be saved for months without going bad. Winter squash takes 80 to 100 days to mature.

There are many types of tomatoes to choose from. Large ones such as: Big Boy, Big Girl, Rutgers, Beefsteak, and small ones such as: Tiny Tim, Cherry, and Roma VF.

WINTER
SQUASH

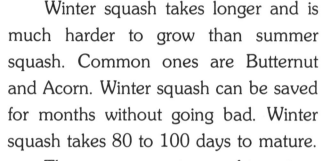

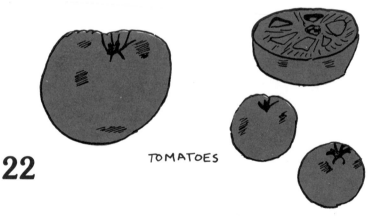

TOMATOES

Tomatoes are found in every home garden. They are easy to grow once the plants are started. You can buy started plants at a garden center. If you want to start your own, you can do this without too much trouble. Start them indoors 8 weeks before planting them outside. Pick tomatoes as they turn red. Tie the plants to a stake to save space. Tomatoes take 55 to 80 days to mature, depending on variety.

Watermelon is very hard to grow. I would stay away from growing it until I had had several years of gardening or was ready for a challenge, if I were you. It can be started indoors 4 weeks before planting outdoors to give it a head start. Watermelon needs a lot of space, sun, and most of all, water. It takes 80 days to mature.

WATERMELON

Of course there are many other vegetables to grow. I could not list them all. The ones I did list are the most common ones. Seed catalogs and garden centers carry many more types of vegetables and also can help you decide what to grow.

This is a list of the easy-to-grow vegetables. When deciding what to grow, use this list to help you. All of these vegetables are good for your first garden. After you are able to grow these varieties you can try harder ones:

bush beans   peas
beets   radishes
carrots   cucumbers
leaf lettuce   summer squash
                    tomatoes*

   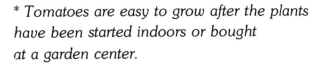

* Tomatoes are easy to grow after the plants have been started indoors or bought at a garden center.

6

WHEN SHOULD
I PLANT?

The time for planting indoors and out-doors is more important then you may think. Planting indoors will be talked about in the next section.

Different vegetables should be planted outdoors at different times. Some vegetables, such as spinach and lettuce, like cool weather and should be planted in early spring and late summer. Other vegetables, such as tomatoes and peppers, like warm weather and should not be planted outside until all chances of frost are past.

This chart divides the United States into four sections. It shows approximately the time of the last killing frost in each area. Find your state on the map. Match the color of your state with the color in the key at the bottom. This will show about when you may expect the last killing frost in your area.

 MAY 1 — JUNE 1   MARCH 1 — APRIL 1

  APRIL 1 — MAY 1   FEB. 1 — MARCH 1

The last killing frost for Connecticut, where I live, is about May 15. This chart would help you to decide when to plant each vegetable if you live in Connecticut.

PLANTING CHART

4-6 weeks before last frost, or April 1	2-4 weeks before last frost, or April 15
broccoli	beets
cabbage	brussels sprouts
lettuce	carrots
peas	celery
spinach	radishes

date of the last frost, or May 15	2-3 weeks after last frost, or June 1
beans	cantaloupe
corn	cucumbers
pumpkins	eggplants
squash	peppers
	tomatoes
	watermelon

27

If you live outside of Connecticut and you want to find out the planting date, look at the chart on page 27 or use a calendar and count back the weeks to find the correct planting dates for your area. For example, if you live in Virginia, the last frost is April 1 to May 1, let's say April 15. You want to plant radishes. Count back three weeks from that date and you will have March 22 or 23.

Do not decide when to plant by the map and chart alone. You have to decide yourself when it is safe to plant. Sometimes the last frost comes early and sometimes it comes late. Do not get fooled by the first nice day in spring. The next day could be cold again. Your parents or neighbors who have gardens can help you decide exactly when to plant. If there is a farm in the area, a farmer could be of help.

28   You will notice that early crops,

such as lettuce, radishes, peas, and spinach, will die as the weather gets warmer. They can be planted again late in August when the weather starts to get cooler.

Here is a chart showing approximately the weeks of the spring months. Use a calendar if you want to. Count backward or forward from last frost date.

MARCH	APRIL	MAY	JUNE
1 8 15 22 29	5 12 19 26	3 10 17 24 31	7 14 21 28

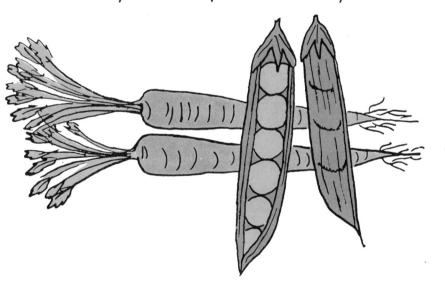

7

WHAT ABOUT STARTING SEEDS INDOORS?

Some vegetables, such as cabbage or broccoli, can be started indoors to give them a head start. Other vegetables, such as peppers, eggplant, and tomatoes, cannot be planted right in the garden. They need a head start of 6 to 10 weeks indoors before they can be planted outdoors.

You can buy these plants from a garden center. They are already started

and are all set to be planted in the

ground. If you want to, you can grow them yourself.

It is easier to buy your plants than to grow them yourself. But if you want to grow them yourself, I will explain how in this chapter.

I would recommend a year or two of gardening before trying to grow your plants indoors. But if you are eager to try, go right ahead. Good luck to you. You will most likely make some mistakes, and some of your plants will die, but that is all part of gardening. It took

about four years before I was able to start plants indoors that were successful.

Different plants should be started indoors at different times, before planting outdoors. This chart shows when to start each of the following plants indoors:

Vegetable	Start plants indoors before planting outdoors:
eggplant	8-10 weeks
pepper	8-10 weeks
tomato	6-8 weeks
broccoli	4-6 weeks
cauliflower	4-6 weeks
cabbage	4-6 weeks
brussels sprouts	4-6 weeks
head lettuce	4-6 weeks
* cantaloupe	3-4 weeks
* watermelon	3-4 weeks
* squash	3-4 weeks

You do not have to start these plants indoors unless you live way up north where the growing season is very short. But if you want to give them a head start, you can start them indoors.

If you start your plants too soon, they will get too big and not have many leaves on them. The word *leggy* is used to describe older plants like this. When a leggy plant is planted outside, it will not grow as well as a younger plant. A younger plant is always better to plant in the ground than an older plant.

A YOUNG PLANT

AN OLDER LEGGY
PLANT

33

You will now need soil to start your plants in. Seed 'n Start kits already have soil in them. They are little kits that give you about 12 compartments for your seeds. The kit is filled with soil and comes with seeds. This is the easiest way to start seeds. If you are starting seeds for the first time, I would strongly recommend Seed 'n Start kits.

If you are not using Seed 'n Start kits, you will need soil to start your seeds in. You should not use soil from the garden. You need a special growing soil. You can buy this soil already made, or you can make it yourself. To make your own starting soil you should use the following:

    one part potting soil
    one part sphagnum peat moss
    one part vermiculite or perlite

All of this soil is sterilized if bought at a garden center or store. Vermiculite and perlite are spongy and they hold water. They also provide air spaces in the soil. The sphagnum peat moss provides extra nutrients to the soil.

You now need something to plant in. You can use peat pots. Peat pots are made of compacted peat moss and can be planted right into the ground. Plastic trays can also be used. Any small container can be used to start seeds indoors as long as it has holes at the bottom for drainage. If you look around the house, you will find many types of containers to start seeds in.

You may decide to plant your seeds in flats. A *flat* is any type of tray used to start plants in. The flat must have holes in the bottom for drainage. This is for any extra water that the plant does not soak up. Seeds planted in flats are later transplanted to their own containers.

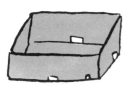

You can also start plants in containers that they will stay in. Either way is fine, but I recommend starting them in flats. You should be able to start your plants indoors without any trouble if you follow these simple steps:

1. Fill the containers that the seeds are going to be started in with the starting soil described earlier.

2. If starting in flats, sprinkle seeds on top of the soil and cover with about ¼ inch of soil. If started in containers where they will stay, plant 3 or 4 seeds in each container.

3. Water seeds. At first give your seeds a lot of water. This is to get the soil wet. It is usually very dry before it is used.

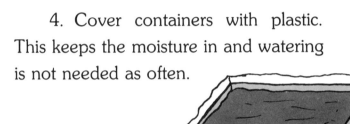

4. Cover containers with plastic. This keeps the moisture in and watering is not needed as often.

5. Place containers in a warm, dark place for faster sprouting. The words *sprouting* and *germinating* mean starting to grow.

37

6. When the seeds sprout, put them near a sunny window. A window on the south side of the house would be the best. You can also grow your plants under fluorescent plant lights. The lights should be turned on for 12 hours a day. The plastic should be removed when the first plants grow tall enough to push against it.

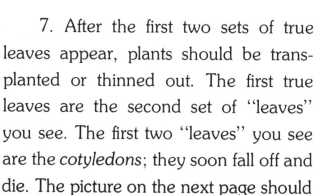

7. After the first two sets of true leaves appear, plants should be transplanted or thinned out. The first true leaves are the second set of "leaves" you see. The first two "leaves" you see are the *cotyledons*; they soon fall off and die. The picture on the next page should be helpful in understanding this.

38

first set of true leaves

cotyledons —

— second set of true leaves

8. If plants were started in flats, they should now be transplanted to their own containers. They can be planted in peat pots, clay pots, plastic pots, or even paper cups (with holes punched in the bottom). You should carefully take out the best plants from the flat with a small spoon and plant each in its own container. If the plant is tall, plant it a little deeper. Lightly pack down soil around plant with your fingers.

39

9. If you started your plants in the containers they will stay in, you will have to thin them out. *Thinning* means removing some young plants to give room to stronger plants. You should thin out your plants until you have one plant per pot. If the container is large, you can leave more than one plant. The best way to thin out your young plants is to cut out the ones you do not want with a pair of scissors. This way the roots of the other plants are not bothered. Clip the plants close to the soil.

10. Water your plants every day or when the soil feels dry.

About a week before you are going to plant your plants outside, they will have to be hardened off. *Hardening off* means getting plants used to the outdoors. This is done in the following way:

1. Nine or ten days before planting outside, take plants outside in the daytime.

2. Bring plants inside at night.

3. Cut down on the amount you water your plants at this time.

4. After about six or seven days, leave plants outside overnight.

5. On the tenth day or so, plant your plants in the ground.

If you find that your plants are not growing very well outside, or for example, if they get white spots on them, bring them inside and start over again. White spots are frostbite.

8

HOW DO I PLANT OUTDOORS?

In the last chapter we talked about planting indoors. In this chapter we will talk about planting outdoors.

Before you do the planting in the garden, you should plan the garden on paper. To help you to decide where to plant everything, here are a few things you should know.

Plant the taller plants on the north side of the garden and the shorter plants on the south side of the garden. This

42

prevents the plants from shading each other.

Marigolds can be planted between tomato plants. They help to keep away the bugs, who do not like the smell.

Early crops, such as radishes, lettuce, peas, and spinach, should all be planted near each other. This way, when they die in the summer, they can be re-

43

placed with something like beans or tomatoes. You can also plant lettuce, spinach, radishes, and peas in a shaded part of the garden.

I have made some sample garden plans to help you see how it is done. Notice the way the earlier crops are together and the taller crops are also together.

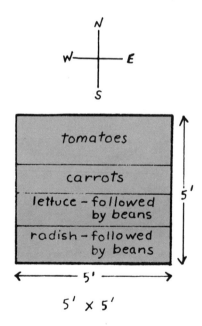

5' × 5'

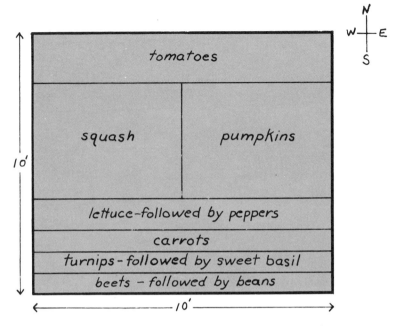

These charts can be made to scale on graph paper. You can very easily make up your own scale. Use one box as 1 square inch or 1 square foot, depending on the size of your garden and graph paper.

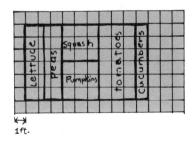

1ft.

45

When planting the seeds, do not plant in wet or damp soil. When wet soil dries, it becomes packed and the young plants have trouble breaking the surface.

Most of the vegetables are best planted in rows. This can be done by following these simple steps:

1. You can make straight rows by putting a stick into the ground at both ends of the garden and running a string between them.

2. Use a hoe or shovel to make a shallow trench under the string.

3. Plant small seeds ¼ inch deep or just below the surface.

4. Plant large seeds 1 inch deep.

5. Plant seeds 1 inch apart. Seeds should be thinned out later according to the instructions on the seed packets.

6. Pack soil down lightly around the seeds.

Some vegetables, such as pumpkins, cucumbers, squash, and even corn, can be planted in hills or small mounds. Follow these easy steps for planting in hills:

47

1. Make a small mound of soil about 1 foot across and about 2 inches high.

2. The hills should be 2 feet apart each way.

3. Plant 5 or 6 seeds in each hill.

4. Thin out to 2 or 3 plants per hill.

I have made a chart to help you to decide how to plant seeds—how deep, how far apart, and how much space to leave between rows.

SEED PLANTING CHART

Vegetable	planting depth	space between plants	space between rows
beans	1″	4″	18″
beets	½″	4″	1′
broccoli	¼″	1′	18″
brussels sprouts	½″	1′	18″
cabbage	¼″	18″	2′
cantaloupe	½″	6″	hills 3′
carrots	¼″	4″	1′
corn	1″	8″	2′
cucumbers	½″	6″	hills 3′
eggplant	¼″	1′	2′
lettuce	¼″	8″	18″
peas	1″	4″	1′
peppers	¼″	1′	18″
pumpkin	1″	6″	hills 4′
radishes	¼″	2″	1′
spinach	¼″	8″	18″
squash	1″	8″	hills 4′
tomatoes	¼″	18″	2′
watermelon	½″	8″	hills 4′

You already know about hardening off plants you have begun indoors before you move them outside. When you buy plants at a garden center they will have been hardened off before they were sold.

Your pre-started plants—whether you grow them yourself or buy them at a store—will have to be removed from their trays. If your plants are in peat pots, peal down the sides of the pot when planting.

If your plants are in plastic trays, the plants can be separated with a fork and scooped out. Be careful separating the plants. The less root disturbance the better.

If your plants are in small plastic cups or clay pots, water the plants a little and turn the pot upside down. While holding the plants between your fingers, tap them out. *Tapping out* means tapping the pot gently, which helps separate the soil from the edge of the pot.

Plant your plants deep enough so that the soil barely touches the first leaves. If the plant is tall without very many leaves, then plant it deeper. You can even lay the plant on its side if you have to.

9

WATERING AND THINNING OUT.

Your vegetable garden should be watered in the morning or at dinner time. This way the water will soak into the ground, and the roots will get a chance to drink it. If you water your garden in the middle of the day, the sun will dry it up before the roots get the water.

52

You do not have to water every day if it has been raining. In August, when it gets very dry and it doesn't rain much, you will have to water more often. Most vegetables will grow very well with a lot of water.

Thinning or thinning out is a very important part of vegetable gardening. You had to thin out the young plants in pots, and you also have to thin them when you plant outdoors. Young plants grow fast and need food and space to mature properly.

Seed packets usually tell you how far apart to thin each plant. You may think that it is mean to pull out the young plants and throw them away. You don't

have to throw them away, though. The young plants can be carefully dug up and transplanted somewhere else in the garden. You can also throw them in your compost pile if you have one.

10

I HATE WEEDING!

I hate weeding too! Weeds will grow in every home garden. Weeds will grow faster if the garden is not mulched in any way. *Mulching* means covering the ground with mulch to control weeds and keeping the soil moist. Mulch includes compost, grass clippings, plastic sheets, cardboard, and even newspaper. If mulching with newspaper, cardboard, or plastic sheets, you will have to have rocks at the corners to hold the mulch down.

Weeds soak up a lot of water that is given to the plants. They take up a lot of space. They also use a lot of the food **55** in the soil. The best way to get rid of a weed is to pull it out or dig it out by hand. A hoe can also be used. If you get all the roots, the weed will not grow back.

It is much easier to pull weeds when the ground is wet. After a rain is the best time to weed. The soil is softer and the weeds come up with less work. If the weeds are close to the plants, be careful. While pulling out the weed, you could disturb the plant's roots.

This is a good time to talk about staking plants and growing plants on fences. Tomato plants should be staked to save space in the garden and to keep plants off the ground. If tomatoes are grown on the ground, they will rot more easily. If you decide not to stake your tomato plants, you should move toma-toes themselves around every other day.

This way the tomatoes will not be touching the ground in the same spot and they will not rot or get wormy.

Pumpkins, cucumbers, and some squash (winter) can be grown so that they climb on fences or trestles to save space. Pole beans, peas, and lima beans can be grown on strings, small fences, or chicken wire. Chicken wire is excellent

for growing vegetables on. It can be bought at a lumber store for a reasonable price.

Well, here we are at the end of the book. Now you are all ready to start your garden. Be patient, and don't expect everything to grow the day after you plant. It takes time. Welcome to the wonderful world of gardening. Most of all,
GOOD LUCK!!!

IRENE INGLE PUBLIC LIBRARY